D0343823

LADYBIRD BOOKS
UK | USA | Canada | Ireland | Australia
India | New Zealand | South Africa

Ladybird Books is part of the Penguin Random House group of companies
whose addresses can be found at global.penguinrandomhouse.com.
ladybird.com

First published 2015
001

Text and illustrations copyright © Astley Baker Davies Ltd/Entertainment One UK Ltd, 2015
Adapted by Lauren Holowaty

This book is based on the TV series *Peppa Pig*
Peppa Pig is created by Neville Astley and Mark Baker
Peppa Pig © Astley Baker Davies Ltd/Entertainment One UK Ltd 2003
www.peppapig.com

Ladybird and the Ladybird logo are registered or unregistered
trademarks owned by Ladybird Books Ltd

Printed in China

A CIP catalogue record for this book is available from the British Library

ISBN: 978-0-241-20150-3

Peppa's Post

One day, Mr Zebra the Postman delivered a very important letter to Peppa and George's house.

"Look, George!" cried Peppa, running to the front door. "It's for us."
"Snort! Snort!" grunted George excitedly.
"I wonder what's inside," said Peppa.

"It's your tickets for Mr Potato's marvellous theatre show," said Mummy Pig, helping Peppa open the envelope.

"Oooh, goody!" gasped Peppa. "I love the theatre, and I love Mr Potato."

That afternoon, Mummy and Daddy Pig drove Peppa and George to the Grand Theatre to meet Madame Gazelle and their friends.

When they arrived, the show was about to start.
"Please welcome," said a loud voice, "your friend and mine . . . MR POTATO!"
"Oooh! Wow!" the children gasped all the way through the show.
After it finished, they gave Mr Potato a huge round of applause, and Madame Gazelle gave everyone a special envelope to take home.

Daddy Pig helped Peppa and George read their letter from Madame Gazelle. The next morning, they followed the map to playgroup.

"Welcome, little ones!" Madame Gazelle beamed, after the mummies and daddies had left. "Today we are putting on a pantomime, and there will be a special guest coming."

"OOOOOOH!" everyone gasped.

"Now, children," continued Madame Gazelle, "we have lots to do. First, we must make the posters and invitations for the pantomime."

When they'd finished, everyone gave their invitations to Mr Zebra. He raced off to deliver them. The first one was for Mummy and Daddy Pig . . .

Mummy and Daddy Pig
The Little House
On Top of the Hill

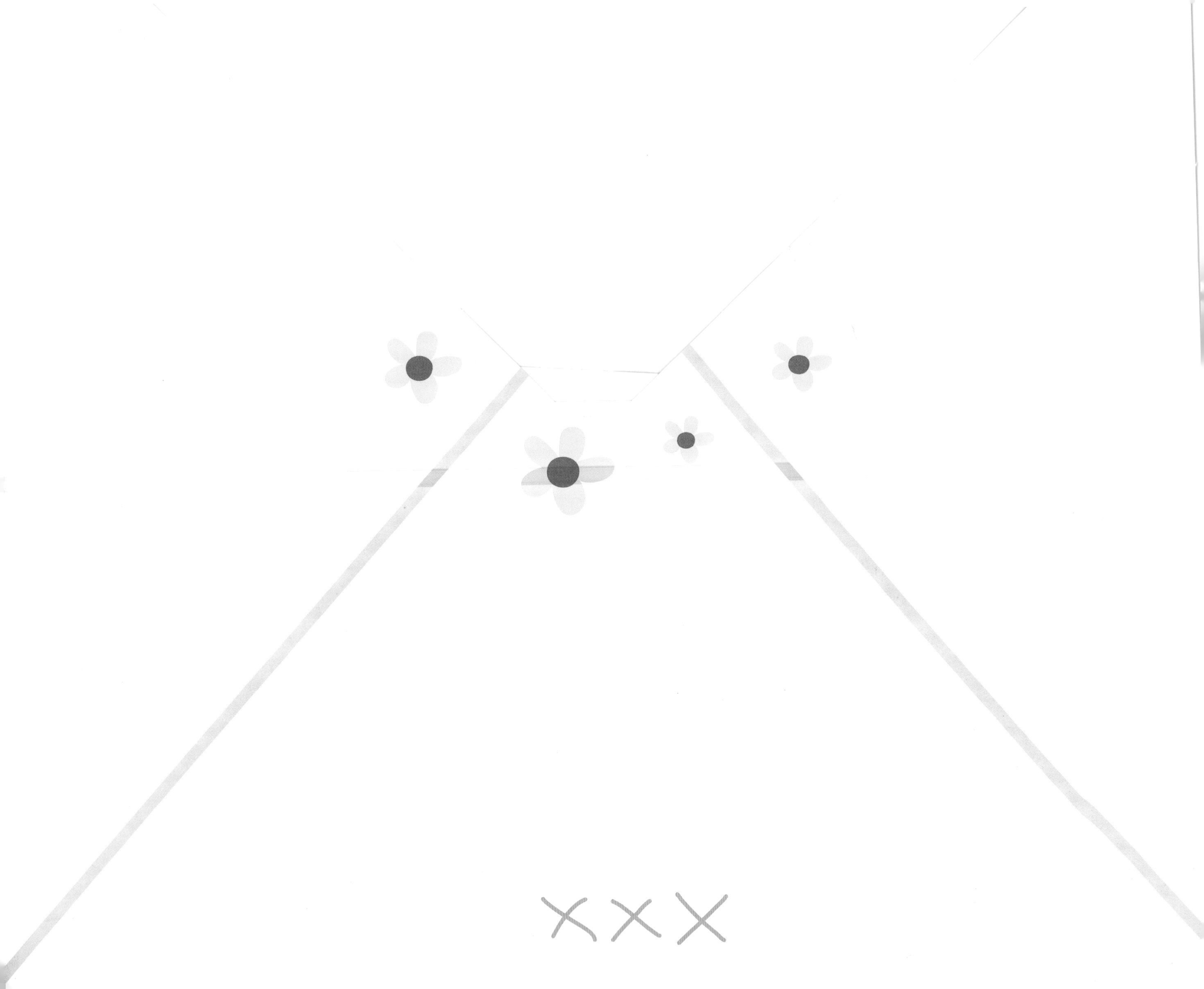
XXX

Mr Zebra handed Mummy and Daddy Pig
their invitation to the pantomime.
"How lovely," said Mummy Pig, when
she opened the envelope. "Of course we
can come."

Mummy and Daddy Pig gave their reply to Mr Zebra,
and he raced off to deliver the other invitations.

Later that morning, the playgroup doorbell rang. DING-DONG! It was Mr Zebra, with an enormous parcel for all the children.

"It's a dressing-up box," Peppa whispered to Suzy. "A very big one." "Your costumes are here, my little stars!" announced Madame Gazelle.

The dressing-up box was full of wonderful costumes! Peppa and her friends picked their outfits and got ready.

"Now you must practise your lines," said Madame Gazelle. "Peppa, you can start."

"I'm Little Red Riding Hood," began Peppa. "I'm going to visit my grandma. Snort!"

Danny Dog was dressed as the Big Bad Wolf.
"I'm going to eat Little Red Riding Hood. Woof!" he barked.

"Wonderful acting, Peppa and Danny!"
said Madame Gazelle.
The children were still practising when
the doorbell rang again. DING-DONG!
"It's Mr Zebra, with more post!"
announced Madame Gazelle.

The children opened the parcel and found replies to their invitations.

"Fabulous news!" exclaimed Madame Gazelle. "Everyone can come to our pantomime. Even our mystery guest."

"Who is the mystery guest, Madame Gazelle?" asked Peppa. "Is it the Queen?"

"You'll have to wait and see," replied Madame Gazelle.

"Oh," sighed Peppa, a little disappointed.

It was almost time for the pantomime to start. Everyone was arriving.

Peppa peered round the curtain.
She could see the mummies and daddies, but she couldn't see a mystery guest.
"Please find your programmes and take your seats," said Madame Gazelle.
"Our pantomime is about to begin."

"Ladies and gentleman," said Madame Gazelle, "welcome to our pantomime!"

The children leapt on to the stage and everyone stood up to take photos. Click, click! Flash, flash!

"Please!" said Madame Gazelle. "For the sake of the actors, no photography!"

The parents quietly sat back down in their chairs and the show began.

"I'm Little Red Riding Hood," began Peppa. "I'm visiting my grandma."

"I'm the Big Bad Wolf," said Danny. "I'm pretending to be Grandma, then I'm going to eat everyone!"
"I'm the hunter," said Pedro. "I'm chasing the Big Bad Wolf away!"
"Oooh! Wow!" the parents gasped all the way through the performance.

When the pantomime finished, the children bowed. Everyone gave them a huge round of applause.

Except for Mr Zebra, who was so tired from delivering all the letters that he had fallen fast asleep!
"Where's the mystery guest?" Peppa whispered to Suzy.

Just then, the clapping stopped and a loud voice said, "Please welcome our special guest, your friend and mine . . ."

"MR POTATO!"

"Mr Potato is more famous than the Queen!" whispered Peppa excitedly.

"What a marvellous performance!" said Mr Potato, leaping up from his hiding place next to the stage. "This pantomime was the best I've ever seen!"

"Hooray!" cheered the children. They loved their pantomime, but they loved meeting Mr Potato even more!

Hee!

Hee!

Hee!

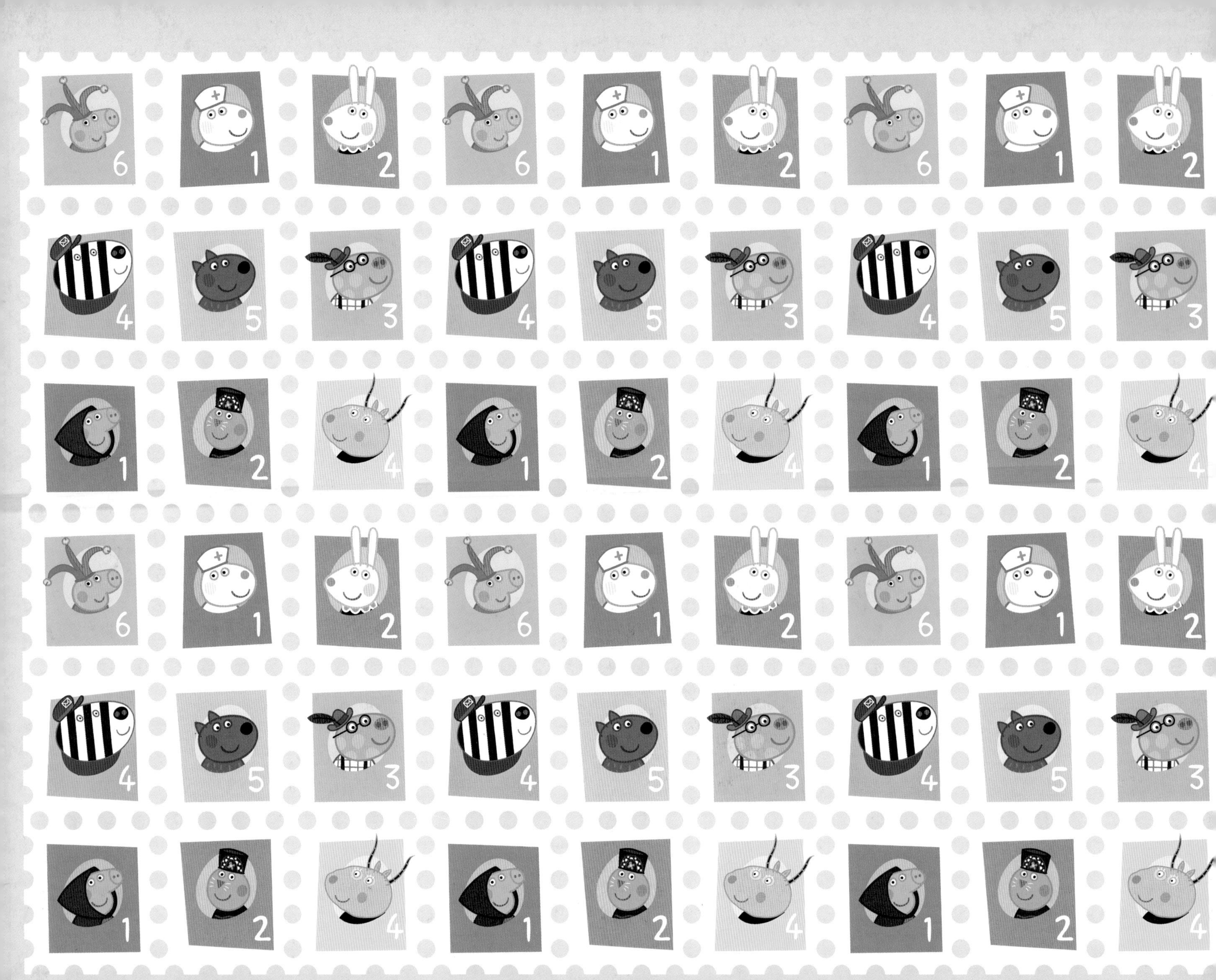